Princess
Says Goodnight

Princess Says Goodnight

NAOMI HOWLAND

Illustrated by
DAVID SMALL

HARPER
An Imprint of HarperCollinsPublishers

To a royal group of women—
Anita, Lisze, Marla, Mary Ann, & Nancy
—N.H.

To Lily
—D.S.

At the palace in the nighttime,

when Princess leaves the ball,

is she practicing her curtsies
while dancing down the hall?

Will she hold a candelabra
while climbing up the stairs

and have a frothy glass of milk
with chocolate cream éclairs?

Does she look out from her tower
just to count up all her sheep?

Will she make a wish upon a star
before she goes to sleep?

When she removes her slippers,
to make their clear glass shine,

does she rub them with a hankie
of an elegant design?

When Princess takes a bubble bath,
what do you suppose?

She has a special fluffy towel
for each one of her toes.

Is her favorite princess color
for all her royal clothes

every pretty shade of pink—
mauve and peach and rose?

Will Princess wear a bathrobe
made of silken lacy flounce,

the kind that loses feathers
with each and every bounce?

Does Daddy check the mattress
for peas and other lumps?

Will her mom fluff up her pillows
and smooth out any bumps?

Does she brush her hair and floss her teeth,
and then climb into bed

and give her little froggy, Prince,
a kiss upon the head?

Will her fine ladies-in-waiting
sing a lullaby duet

while the jester and the footmen
form a barbershop quartet?

Will Princess hang her tiara
on the bedpost overnight?

Does she get a bedtime story
before turning off the light?

Yes she does, and a big kiss, too.
And then she says,

Library of Congress Cataloging-in-Publication Data

Howland, Naomi.

    Princess says goodnight / by Naomi Howland ; illustrated by David Small. — 1st ed.

        p.   cm.

    Summary: Rhyming text presents what a princess might do between leaving the ball and saying goodnight.

    ISBN 978-0-06-145525-4 (trade bdg.) — ISBN 978-0-06-145526-1 (lib. bdg.)

    [1. Stories in rhyme.   2. Princesses—Fiction.   3. Bedtime—Fiction.]   I. Small, David, date, ill.   II. Title.

PZ8.3.H843Pri   2011   2009023550

[E]—dc22   CIP

                                                                                                                                          AC

Typography by Martha Rago

10 11 12 13 14 15   SCP   10 9 8 7 6 5 4 3 2 1

First Edition